THE
ARRANGEMENT
VOL. 4

H.M. Ward

www.SexyAwesomeBooks.com

Laree Bailey Press

Laree Bailey Press
First Print Edition: May 2013
ISBN: 978-0615827506

THE
ARRANGEMENT
VOL. 4

CHAPTER 1

The city has that scent in the air, like it's going to snow. Wrapping my arms tighter around my middle, I walk down the street. The sidewalks have an inky sheen, as if it's been misting. Car horns blare as I breathe in the exhaust and try to fathom what happened, but I don't know. I can't grasp it. The look on Sean's face, the way his voice sounded...

My stomach twists like I'm going to be sick. I gave him my heart and he fucking returned me—like I was broken. Like he didn't want me. Maybe throwing all the cash at Sean was stupid, but I had to do it. I don't turn back. I don't look behind me. I already know Sean isn't there. He doesn't love me.

As I walk along the sidewalk in a daze, a car rolls up next to me. It's late. I don't notice at first. It isn't until the window rolls down and I hear a voice that I turn and glance at the car. The wind whips my hair, sending the strands flying every which way. My heels are in my hand. I'm walking along wearing nothing on my feet but stockings. The cold ground burns through the silk. It's one of the only things I can feel in the storm of pain. It's consuming me, swallowing me whole.

This is why I had no relationships. I lied to myself and said I avoided relationships because my schedule didn't permit it, but that wasn't true. I dodged relationships, because my heart couldn't take it. I've lost enough people to make anyone lose their freaking mind, but somehow I manage to keep going.

"Miss Stanz," a male voice calls from the car.

I can see his face through the open window. He's one of the guys that were with Miss Black the first time Sean set off my bracelet.

I stare at him. The wind stings my eyes, making them water, but I don't blink. The car stops rolling and the man steps out a moment later. He's enormous, all muscle and strength. I say nothing.

His eyes sweep over my face like he knows what made me like this. "Are you hurt?" I shake my head. He reaches forward for my shoes. I hand them over. Then, he extends his elbow like a gentleman and escorts me to the car.

As we slip into the backseat, he reminds me, "You can't leave the premises without notifying our employer. You were lucky last time." His tone changes and I know that I'm in trouble.

One time is forgivable, but two times is not. I just nod and stare out the window.

The man doesn't say much until we're approaching Miss Black's building. "Listen, I don't know what your story is or why you did what you did, but this job isn't for people who can't hold their shit together.

It's an act. The women who understand that survive. The ones who don't learn that lesson get crippled. There's no such thing as 'just sex,' Miss Stanz. At the same time, that's what you need to think in order to excel at this job."

I blink at him. Surprise flashes across my face. Why is he telling me this? "Am I that transparent?"

The corner of his mouth pulls up. *Apparently so.* He tells me, "You can't fall in love with them. You won't make it. Figure out a way to harden your heart. Don't let them in, ever."

The car has stopped. Taking a deep breath, I lean forward to get out. I look at the guy and say, "Thank you."

"For what?" he asks. The expression on his face says that the other girls don't talk to him much. He seems surprised that I said anything.

I shrug. "For finding me and helping me out. I'm not cut out for this, but there's no other way."

His dark eyes seem too gentle for someone so thuggish looking. He glances at the building and then back at me. I get the feeling that he shouldn't be talking to me at all, never mind telling me what he's about to say. "When you go inside, Black is going to reprimand you. Take it. Don't blubber or give her any backtalk and she'll keep you around. Make excuses and she'll kick you to the curb." He doesn't say anything else. Instead, he pulls the car door open and exits to the sidewalk.

I slip out after him and give a subtle nod of thanks. I can't lose this job. He hands me my heels and I slip them back on. My stockings are ruined. There are runs up the legs from walking around barefoot.

Taking a deep breath, I walk into the building and head to the elevator. I steel myself. Black's going to be pissed. I decide to follow the guard's instructions. I can't get fired. I can't. My nerves are beyond shot. I feel numb, like I've been slapped one too many times. Life keeps bitch-slapping me, but I keep getting up.

The elevator takes me up and stops at the seventeenth floor. I step off and walk into the office. There are hardly any lights on. I make my way to the back, to Miss

Black's desk. I turn to walk into her office, but no one is there.

Someone clears their throat behind me. I whirl around and see Black sitting on the couch with a cup of coffee in her hands. Her slender legs are crossed at the knee. She looks regal, and pissed. "Never—and I mean never—has a client called and requested a different girl. What did you do, Avery? What could you have possibly done that upset the client so much that he tossed you out in the middle of your appointment?" Her dark eyes are hard. They bore into me like I'm the most irritating person she's ever met. She works her jaw. I can tell Miss Black wants to scream, but she restrains herself.

Apathy. I need to not care. I need to say it's my fault and convince her that I won't mess up anything else. My gaze is on the carpet. I don't look up as I speak. "It was my fault. I did something that reminded Mr. Ferro of someone. It unnerved him. There's no excuse for it. I take full responsibility for my actions."

This isn't what she expected to hear. Black puts down her mug and sits up straight, unfolding her legs as she does so. "You remind him of someone?" I nod. "How do you know?"

"He told me the night before."

Black is quiet for a moment. Her eyes sweep over me as she thinks. I can tell she still wants to chew me out. "Why didn't you wait at the hotel for the car? After Mr. Ferro called me, I hung up and called you. You didn't answer your phone and you left the grounds. I had to send Gabe to find you."

I swallow hard. I don't know what to say, so I tell her the truth. "I didn't know what to do. It's my fault. I didn't answer my phone, because I was afraid you were going to fire me." Black stares at me. I feel her gaze on my face. Her anger is palpable. It hangs in the air, thick as the evening fog. I finally look up at her. "I need this job."

Miss Black stands and walks up to me. Her arms are folded across her chest. Her eyes narrow to slits, so that I can barely see her eyes. She's like a tiger waiting to rip me to shreds, but I don't cower. I don't back down. Her voice is level when she asks, "Why should I keep you?"

Desperation climbs up my throat and chokes me. This is it. She's going to fire my ass and there's nothing that I can do about it. I'll be living in a cardboard box with a broken heart for the rest of my life. I can't process this. I can't grasp the size of my mistake, my mistake of trusting Sean, of telling how I felt. I poured out my soul and he acted like I puked on his shoes. My mouth goes dry. I lick my lips and form an answer in my mind.

When I speak, I sound like I'm begging, probably because I am. My voice comes out in a rush. "Because I'll do anything. Because I won't remind everyone of someone they loved. Because—"

Miss Black cuts me off, "Oh Avery, shut up." Black pinches the bridge of her nose as though she has the world's worst headache.

My heart pounds harder. Could this get more fucked up than it already is? I can't get fired, I just can't. I see my life ending and everything I worked so hard for fluttering away. I swallow hard.

Her dark eyes are narrowed like she wants to rip my head off. She stares at me like that for a few moments. Then she unfolds her arms that were plastered tightly to her chest. Taking my chin in her hands, Black tilts my face up so that our gazes connect. "I should fire you for this. I should let you go without a penny and not feel one bit of remorse."

I look into her eyes wondering how she got to where she is now. I wonder about the guy that got away. I wonder if she's alone because she wants to be or if it's because this job fucked with her mind and not just her body. It's a price that I didn't consider. I never thought I'd fall in love. I never thought things could come to this.

I inhale slowly and resist the urge to ball my fingers into fists. My world is falling apart. I need this job, but I won't beg again. We stare each other down. I don't look away and neither does she. Neither of us speaks. It's like a showdown and I know that at any second, Black will draw and I'll be dead. There are no more chances. I blew it. I messed up and this is the price. Miss Black presses her eyes shut and sighs. When she looks at me again, her livid expression softens. She shakes her head and her arms fall to her sides. The fight spills from her body and I can finally breathe again.

Miss Black paces away from me and pours herself more coffee. Without looking up, she says, "It would be a pity to throw you away. There's such potential. I see it in your eyes." She turns, stirring the hot liquid and regards me. "But, you're a hollow shell. The only thing keeping your neck above water is your defiance, your utter refusal to give up. If you gave that last piece of resistance to me, I could turn your life into a dream, but you're insolent, Avery. I told you to keep your personal life out of this." Black takes a sip of the coffee in her hands and then sets it down. She paces, thinking.

Every inch of my body is fighting me. I want to scream that it isn't my fault. I want to say that Sean duped me, that he made me think he cared, but he doesn't. All those words are toxic. If I say them, I'll never work for Miss Black again, so I work my jaw and try not to react. I wonder if she knows the extent of my stupidity—I wonder if Sean told her what I said. Panic races through my veins, but I stay still. I keep the fear from clouding my eyes with tears. I lock it down and bite my tongue before I can do any more damage.

Miss Black's frustrated gaze cuts to mine, and she stops in her tracks. Pointing a perfectly manicured finger at me, she says, "You will do exactly what I tell you. You will take the clients that I give you and thank me for it. You have no say in anything anymore. Do you understand?" I nod, even though I'm not sure what she intends to do with me. I know I'm lucky, though.

Something in Miss Black's gaze changes and I know she's decided to keep me around. She extends her hand to me. "Give back the money from tonight, and let's move on."

Damn. She can't be serious. My face pinches in confusion. "Give it back?"

Black snaps her fingers and thrusts her hand at me. "Yes. You didn't finish your job. You can't honestly tell me that you think you should be paid as if you did?" She arches an eyebrow at me and wiggles her fingers impatiently, waiting for me to slap the cash in her hand.

I need this job, but I can't fathom not getting paid. I mean to control my temper, but I can't. I step toward her and look down at her palm, and then up into her face. "Yes, I think I should be paid and the reason is really simple—he fucked me. He used me more than once. I was with him for two nights, letting him have his way with me. To reiterate—he had sex with me and yes, I want to be paid for that." My muscles tense. It's everything I can do to maintain an ounce of composure and not scream in her face.

This is Sean's fault. If he didn't send me back, this wouldn't have happened.

Miss Black looks irritated. She folds her arms back over her chest as I speak. Her neck is gracefully tipped to the side. Black lets me speak, never blinking. The muscle in her jaw twitches, like she wants to yell. She holds up a single finger and responds. "You were with him one night. Tonight, he threw you out and asked for a refund."

I try so hard to contain my anger. It wants to burst from my lips and spew horrible things everywhere. I'm so mad that I'm shaking. I counter, "I'm not a virgin anymore and it's his fault. I can't demand that price again. And I can't help that I reminded Mr. Ferro of the person he was trying to forget. I deserve at least half of my payment."

Black steps toward me with fury in her eyes, but I don't back down. Her nose is a fraction of an inch from mine. "You don't deserve a damn thing. You work here because I say you can. You fuck who I say you will. You have no rights, no recourse. If I don't think you should be paid, you won't be... However, some of your arguments are reasonable. I will let you keep a third of your fee. That's it. Which means the money I gave you tonight needs to be given back."

My heart sinks. The hollow spot in my chest aches. This whole thing makes Sean's rejection so much worse. It hammers in the fact that I'm a whore and I totally pissed off my pimp. What do I do? I glance away, but Black doesn't back off. Sensing that I'll lose this job completely, I give in. I take a breath and let the tension roll out of my shoulders.

I look up at her. "Fine, but I spent the money you gave me. It's already gone."

Black's eyes go wide. It was a lot of cash. "How? You went straight to work." Black's eyes dart to my purse, like she doesn't believe me. It's sitting in the chair across from her desk.

I reach for the handbag and open the top. "Look for yourself. I don't have the money. I spent it all." I hand her my purse, but Black just stares at me. After a second, she takes my bag and looks inside. I have two dollars and some change. Nothing else. I threw the rest of that money in Sean's face.

Black makes a growling sound at the back of her throat. "Fine." She thrusts the purse back at me. "If that's the way you want to play, then you owe me. You'll be working for free until you pay your debt off."

I nod, because that's all I can do. "You'll get back every cent you gave me."

Miss Black laughs. The sound makes my skin crawl. "Yes I will, because if you try to short me, Avery, I will take it out on you in a way that you couldn't possibly fathom." There's darkness in her eyes that sends a chill up my spine.

I believe her.

CHAPTER 2

Two dollars. I only have two dollars, and I have to get by for at least five days. I rest my forehead on the steering wheel of my car. It has a full tank of gas, thank God. I drive back to the dorm with white smoke blowing in my face. The heater isn't on, so I'm not sure what's going on. By the time I pull into a parking spot and stall, I smell like a chimney.

Racing up the stairs, I try to avoid Mel and go straight to my room. But, as I'm fumbling through my bag for the keys she sees me. "Hey, white girl. What are you doing home already? I thought—"

I don't look up at her. I try to find the keys faster, but I can't. Mel is a few steps from me when I finally lose it. Taking the bag, I turn on my heel and hurl it at the wall. Her words stop. Mel stops. She stares at me as I let out a strangled sob, and slam my back into the wall. Sliding down, I hold my face in my hands and the tears start. I wish they wouldn't. Not now. I was almost inside. Almost.

Mel rushes toward me and kneels next to me on the floor. I hear her footfalls and sense her presence, but don't look up. There are more people now. I feel their eyes on me. They linger, staring at the girl having a breakdown in the hallway.

Mel snaps at them, "Move the fuck on. There's nothing to see here." Too many shoes hustle by, muttering under their breath about Mel's manners. Her hand rests gently on my shoulder. "Come on, Avery. Don't do this here. And, you sure as hell can't go into your room. Amber's in there with—God, I don't even want to tell you.

"Just come on. Let's go back to my room for the night. It'll be just me and you. You can stuff your face with ice cream and Ambien. Come on." Mel grabs my arm and pulls me up.

I stand, but it feels like I'm made of paper-thin glass. I wipe the tears streaming down my cheeks with the back of my hand. It leaves a black smear of mascara on my skin. I look like a freaky clown, but I don't care. Mel grabs my purse and picks up the lipstick and other crap that flew out when it hit the wall. Quickly, she gathers my things and then pulls me back to her room. By the time we get there, my face is covered in snot. I want to fall apart. I don't want to keep going anymore. I fall into the chair and bury my face in the arm and never get up.

"Here," Mel hands me a box of tissues. I take them without looking up at her. She sits on the bed, across from me. For a while she says nothing. Then, Mel gets up and takes off her heels and puts away her dress. Water runs for a few minutes and then she comes out of the bathroom. After all that, Mel is in her jammies. She pulls her thick hair into a ponytail as she talks. "You can tell me, you know. I won't judge. God knows, I don't have the right."

I look up at her. My vision is fuzzy. My eyes feel swollen and I can barely swallow. I don't want to talk about it, but I feel like I need to respond. Maybe it'll make me feel better. Maybe. My lips part slowly and the words tumble out. "I told Sean that I loved him."

Mel doesn't react even though I can tell she wants to. Instead, she shifts her legs and presses her lips together, trying not to chew me out. I know she wants to scream at me for being so stupid, but I also know she won't. Mel can tell how close I am to mentally cracking. Her voice is gentle when she asks, "And then what?"

I straighten in my chair and sniffle. Dabbing the tissue to my nose, I shrug and say, "He sent me back."

Mel's head sways as her jaw falls open. "Like, he returned you?"

I smile sadly. "No, it's worse than that. He exchanged me. I said, 'I love you' and he said he wanted a new girl." That scary look on Mel's face is getting worse. Clearing my throat, I choke out, "That's not the worst part."

"Oh shit. What else happened?"

"Before I went to Sean's tonight, Black gave me an advance so that I could buy new clothes. She didn't like that I was wearing the same stuff. She gave me about half of my pay. When things went the way they did, I took the money and threw it in his face. Then, I walked out." I breathe deeply and pinch the bridge of my nose. It feels like my face exploded.

Mel's voice is uncharacteristically quiet, "Black advanced you money and you threw it at the client?" I nod. "And Black wants it back, no doubt." I nod again. "And I assume she fired you?"

"No," my voice is barely a whisper. It scratches out of my throat with a toad-like quality. "I get to work for free until my debt is paid off." I glance over at her, not wanting to, not wanting to see the look on her face.

Mel is rendered speechless for a moment, then everything comes out in a rush. "Avery, you have to go and get that money back from Sean. You don't want things like this. Black's not someone you want to be in debt to. You have to—"

I put up my hand and cut her off. "There is no way in hell that I will ever go back to Sean and beg to get that money back, so you can just stop there."

"Now's not the time for pride, Avery."

"You're wrong, Mel. Now is the time for pride, because it's the only fucking thing I have left. I sold myself to some guy that liked tugging my heartstrings. He made me think that he loved me. He made me think that my whole shitty life..." My voice trails off. I can't finish saying it. Sean gave me a reason to breathe. He gave me something to look forward to, and he lit the embers of hope inside of me. I thought I'd never feel alive again, and now that I do, I want to die. Emotional whiplash isn't for people with broken hearts. I feel like I've been torn apart.

Pressing my fingers to my forehead, I rub little circles and say, "That scrap of pride is all I've got. I'm not going back to him. I'm not talking to him again, ever—for any reason. I'll work it off."

Mel nods, but I can see it on her face—she doesn't approve. She's thinking, trying to help me figure things out. After a second she asks, "How much do you owe? Maybe I can lend you the money. It's better owing me than Black." She knows something that I don't.

I look at her for a moment and shake my head. "It was enough to buy a couple of cars, Mel. Thanks for offering, but I doubt you have it. Plus, you need to pay your bills. This was my mistake. I have to clean it up."

"What's she going to have you do? You know Black's guys do some nasty stuff, right?"

I shrug. "I don't care anymore. I really don't. I okayed the entire sheet, you know." Mel looks shocked. "I said I'd do anything."

"How could you say that?" she squeaks with her jaw hanging open.

I pull my knees into my chest and wrap my arms around my legs. I don't look at her. "How could I not? It doesn't matter. None of this matters."

"Are you listening to yourself? You can't let some dumbass guy ruin your life.

He wanted a fuck and you gave him your heart. He doesn't deserve you, Avery.

"I'm so sorry. I wish I could fix this for you, but telling Black that you'll do anything and everything is a bad plan. There are some sick bastards on her client list. They're too twisted for me, so I know you aren't going to be into it.

"Plus, checking the anything box gets you *anything*. You're not ready for that—and no, you don't want to know what crazy shit they do."

I rub my eyes with the heel of my hands. "What choice do I have?" Mel doesn't answer. I stop rubbing and look up at her.

"Go get the money back from dickwad. Say, 'gimme my money back so I don't have to be a hoe for free.'" I tilt my head to the side and give her an expression that says I'd rather die first. She puffs up. "Well, you realize what it means then, right? That you gave it him for free. If you let Sean keep that money, it's like you fucked him for nothing, and in return he gave you the biggest mind-fuck of your life. Go get your damn money back." Mel is on her feet. She goes to her closet and pulls out a jacket, and stuff hers arms in the sleeves.

"You are not going, so sit down." When she bends over to find her sneakers, I repeat myself, "No. Mel, leave it. Please." I walk up behind her. When Mel turns around, I feel the plea etched into my face. "Leave it alone."

She's mad. I can see the tremor of anger course through her arms. Mel flexes her fingers and lets out a rush of air. Her finger is in my face. She tries to hold it still, but she's so angry. Even though I know she isn't mad at me, it feels like it. She growls at me, "I swear to God, if I see that motherfucker on the street, I'm going to rip his goddamn face off."

The corner of my mouth lifts. "That'd be okay, probably."

Mel snorts. The tension flows out of her back and her hand returns to her side. Mel shakes it off as fast as she can, but I can tell that she still wants to defend me. "I'll give him a tattoo with that pretty carving knife I stole from naked dude." She laughs. It sounds a little crazy, but I laugh, too.

I glance at the door. Her words from before finally sink in. "Did you say someone was in my room with Amber?"

"You know I did, and you don't want to know who. I can't believe it myself." Mel peels off her jacket and throws it into the closet. It lands on the floor. Mel slips off her sneakers and slides the closet doors shut.

"Well, now I have to know."

"No, you don't. It'll make you all sorts of crazy." Mel doesn't meet my gaze. Her eyebrows inch up her forehead and disappear, like she can't believe it. I have a sinking feeling. She knows who it is and doesn't like it. That's why she doesn't want to tell me.

There's only one person we both like and we both thought he was gay. "No," I gasp, with my eyes wide. My hand flies to my mouth as it sinks in. "She's with Marty?"

CHAPTER 3

"Yeah," Mel answers with a strange look on her face. One of her lower eyelids flutters, like she's disgusted. "He's been in there all night. Marty came up the stairs looking for you and stumbled on her."

"How do you know?" I ask, and glance at the door and then back at Mel. "I thought you were going to be out all night."

Mel shrugs. "Black reassigned me at the last second. I thought I was going to be out all night, too. When I got in, I texted M-boy to hang out. He said he was busy.

So, after that I got nothing to do, right, so I figure that rattling the skank-hoe would be fun, so I go down and bang on her door." Mel pauses and folds her arms over her chest. "Guess who answered?"

Shaking my head, I say, "I can't believe it."

"Well, believe it—turns out that Marty-boy is straight, although doing Amber is kind of twisted." Mel is obviously disgusted. Her opinion of Marty just fell about six feet.

I blink a few times. The thought of Amber and Marty is too much. I don't want them together. I don't really think about it, but I find myself on my feet and before I know it, I'm walking down the hall to my room. Mel is on my heels, telling me to think it through, but I don't want to.

They can't!

Stopping in front of my door, I try the knob. It's locked. Odds are the door is blocked, too. I bang on the old wood so hard that the glittery sign Amber has placed above the door falls on my head and then tumbles to the carpet. I can't believe how fast my anger is stoked. Maybe I'm too out of it to do this now, but I can't stop.

Before I know it, I'm pounding the door like a lunatic and screaming, "Open the damn door, Marty! I know you're in there!" I'm practically punching the door when Amber yanks it open.

Amber's eyes dart to my fist and then to Mel. She shrieks and jumps back, like I'm going to slug her in the face. "You said she wasn't coming home! You said you weren't coming home!"

I was nice to her and this is how she repays me. "So, you decided to sleep with my best friend? Just kill me while you're at it! Where is he?" I push past Amber and into the room. Fury is building in my fists. If I don't punch something soon, I'm going to snap. I can't believe Marty. I can't possibly fathom why he'd want Amber.

But when I shove into the room, the sight makes me stop in my tracks. The emotions boiling inside of me don't know where to go, so they come out of my mouth is a strangled sobbing laugh. My mouth gaps open and my fingers try to cover it. I'm stunned into silence.

My side of the room has been barren since I moved in. I couldn't afford to decorate it. After I shove past Amber, I see Marty sitting on my bed—fully clothed—and waving the tips of his fingers at me. The bed he's sitting on isn't mine. I mean, it is, but the bedspread and pillows… OMG. And it doesn't stop there—the walls, the bed, the windows, the nightstand—everything is beautiful.

It's decorated in purples and browns. It's exactly what I would have wanted, but better. Everything is perfect. The bedspread is two-tone raw silk in my favorite shade of lilac. The little lamp on the night stand has a vintage shade with tassels hung from the base. There's a dark chocolate colored frieze rug on the floor, so when I step out of bed in the morning my feet won't get cold.

There's art—a real painting—above my headboard. I have a tufted headboard! My side of the room doesn't look like a prison cell anymore. It's a real bedroom, soft and pretty like Mel's room. The entire time I look around, Mel is muttering obscenities and craning her neck the same way that I am, trying to take it all in.

I can't speak. I can't breathe. My fingers are jammed to my lips as I stare.

"Do you like it?" Marty sounds uncertain, like maybe he shouldn't have done it. "You always said it was lacking, that you would have done something with it." Marty looks at his hands and twists his fingers. "I wanted to give you a present. You've been through hell this week. I thought you were going to be out tonight. I was going to decorate, just slip in and out, but then Amber came in and… well, you came back early." Marty gives me a lopsided smile and stands. Extending his arms, Marty says sheepishly, "Surprise."

I slam my hand against my chest to free the words caught in my throat. My lip trembles when I pull my fingers away. Every bit of my brain is in emotional overload. I can't process what he's done. Pressing my lips together, I try to speak. At first nothing comes out. I clear my throat and try again. "It's beautiful. I love it! I can't believe you did all this!" I run over to Marty and throw my arms around him. He towers over me so that my head is barely at his shoulders. He hugs me and pats my back.

When Marty pulls away, he says, "It's kind of shabby chic meets modern. I didn't know what style you'd like, so I guessed."

I can't stop smiling at him. I run my palm over the bedspread, feeling the soft fabric beneath my hand. "It's perfect. Everything is perfect. I love it! I can't believe you did this for me!"

"You deserve it, kiddo." Marty smiles at me. I can tell that he wants to say more, but Amber is there. His eyes flick over to Mel. "Someone said that work was getting harder and harder. Having something nice to come home to, well, it makes things a little better. And since you've got a good job, I thought you might want to stay for the summer and graduate early. We'd have so much fun."

"You're staying this summer?" I ask, and he nods.

Mel finally speaks up. "You almost made her brain blow up. And holy shit— you need to decorate my room. I would have never put this stuff together and it looks freakin' awesome." Mel's still looking at things with her mouth hanging open— the curtains, the table, the linens. I have linens!

Marty laughs and looks at me. "What'd you think I was doing?" His eyes cut to Amber and he startles. He does a double take. "Oh. Oh!" He smacks me lightly with the back of his hand. "Miss Dirty Brain!"

Amber's voice is hard. She glares at me. "What, you think I said all the crap in the stairwell for—fun?"

I'm glad Amber's nuts. I'm glad she's always the same, always a bit bitchy. My hands fly up, palms facing her. "I don't know my ass from my elbow. Do what makes you happy, Amber, just don't do it on my new bed." I giggle and jump on it and fall back. The throw pillows that were so neatly stacked get squashed under my head, while the rest tumble to the floor.

"Awh, it took twenty minutes to get those just right," Marty whines.

I smile and sink into the new pillows and sigh happily.

"Yeah, but look at her face." Mel says. Her hard edges soften a bit. She glances at

Marty. "You did a good thing, here. I'm glad you weren't doing that thing over there, because I'd have to smack you around with a stupid stick for that." Mel jabs her thumb at Amber.

"I can hear you," Amber sneers as she answers from her bed.

"I know," Mel yells back and rolls her eyes. "I said it loudly, you daft hoe."

Amber mutters something, but I talk over her. "You guys are great. Thank you. I needed this."

Marty grins and claps his hands like he's five. "That's what I was hoping you'd say. You know what happens now, right?" A huge grin sweeps across his face. "Sleepover!"

Amber groans and covers her head with a pillow, while Marty shows me the inflatable beds with matching sheets that he put in one of the drawers under my new bed. We stay up until everyone passes out—everyone except me.

I can't sleep. Every time I close my eyes, I see Sean's face and hear his words, *I'm going to tell Black to send another girl. You can go.*

CHAPTER 4

The days pass slowly with little sleep. It's hump day. Three days since I last saw Sean. Three days since he ripped a hole in my heart. In two days I will work for Miss Black and not get paid. In two days I will pay for my mistakes. I can't think about it. Not now.

I slip out of bed before Amber and jump into the shower. The hot water beats some of the tension out of my sore body. Quietly, I move in the room and get ready for the day. As I dress, I look for my

Mom's cross. I feel myself sinking and I want it. I dig through my jewelry and fail to see the necklace.

The last time I had it was over the weekend at Mom's grave—then the beach. A shiver slips over my spine. If it fell out of my pocket at the beach, I'll never find it again. I dig through my dresser again, but it's not there. A frantic feeling is squeezing my throat. I find the clothes from the beach—still filled with sand—and dig through the pockets. My chest constricts. I can't breathe.

My eyes have the stinging panicky thing going on when Mel pushes the door open. "It's pancake day. Get a move on girl." She snaps her fingers at me. Amber rolls over, muttering nasty comments at Mel. Mel steps inside and finally takes a good look at my face. "What's the matter?"

"I lost my mom's necklace. It isn't here." I clutch my face, trying not to freak out. I turn to Mel and drop my hands to my sides. "I must have dropped it on the beach."

Mel knows how much that necklace means to me. A sad smile softens her features. Mel jerks her head toward the door and says, "No problem. Field 5, here we come."

"But—"

"But nothing, Avery. Come on. I bet we have time to grab some hotcakes to eat in the car. It's not the same thing, but it'll be better than nothing. There's an hour and half before class. We can totally make it there and back in time. Come on." Mel turns and heads out the door.

I'm on her heels. We pretty much run to her car. Mel is wearing a nice pair of jeans with rhinestones on the back pockets and a form fitting sweater that shows off her curves. I'm wearing ratty jeans with holes in the knees, a tank, and my holey sweater. The wind cuts through it, stinging my skin.

Mel takes a fast detour through a McDonald's drive-thru and grabs us breakfast. Then, she speeds out to Jones Beach. The bridges are empty at this time of day. The only people up this early are deer and cops.

Mel stuffs her face with a pancake rolled up like a burrito. When make it to the parking lot, she says, "Okay, we have about 45 minutes before we have to leave. I know where you guys were, but let's start from where you parked and then head out onto the sand." I nod and point to where we parked that day. Mel rolls the car into a slot and kills the engine. We both get out and start looking.

The huge parking lot is empty. The wind blows hard, tangling my hair behind me. When I see the beach, a new set of memories floods my mind. Sean. His hands, his touch. Oh God. I wish I never met him. I wish he ignored me that night, like every other person on that road. Why'd he have to help? Why'd I ever talk to him? Every time I blink, I see Sean's eyes and hear his voice. His smile comes racing back. Everything from the kite hitting his head to the way his lips pressed against mine comes back in a rush.

"You okay there, Avery?" Mel says, staring at me.

My eyes are wide. I haven't blinked. I'm gazing at the sandy boardwalk leading out to the beach. Clutching my hands into fists, I work my jaw and say, "I'm fine. Let's go."

We spend the next hour looking through the sand. Basically, we wander the beach, barefoot and sweep the sand away looking for something silvery and glittering beneath the surface. As it gets closer and closer to time to leave, my heartbeat turns panicked. Where is it? Eventually, I give up trying to locate it with my feet. I'm sifting through the sand on my hands and knees, but I can't find Mom's necklace. It's the last piece of her that I have. My brow is pinched with remorse. It doesn't matter where we look or how far we fan out.

Mom's necklace is gone.

I sit back on my knees and look up at the sky. It's gray with streaky white clouds. Pressing my eyes closed, I stop thinking.

Mel watches me. I feel her eyes on my face. A moment later, she's standing next to me. I feel her hand on my shoulder. I open my eyes and look up at her. "It's not here, Avery."

I stand and brush the sand off my jeans. I'm frozen to the core. I look out at the waves pounding into the sand. I wish my heart would freeze. I wish I didn't feel so much. I can't handle this. I can't bear what my life's become.

Mel snaps her fingers in front of my face. When I don't react, she grabs my shoulders and twists me toward her. "It's not here, but that doesn't mean you won't find it."

"You're too nice." I breathe, still numb.

This can't be happening. My heart races as I glance around, looking at everything, but seeing nothing. Panic is strangling me. I feel it, but I don't let it overcome me even though I want to, even though I feel the need to fall to my knees and scream that life isn't fair. My hysteria gets shoved back into its box. One day it'll spring on someone like a crazed jack-in-the-box and scare the shit out of them.

Mel's laugh pulls me back to the present. I glance at her. Mel has a doubtful smile on her face. "Too nice? That's not something I hear every day." Mel sighs. Tilting her head, she says, "Come on. Nothing good is going to come from sitting out here and freezing our asses off. Let's go to class. I'll help you pull apart your room later. I bet it fell behind the dresser or some dumb shit." Mel's words are kind, but I hear it in her voice—she knows I lost it. She knows the necklace will never been seen again, and she's worried about me. She thinks I'm coming unglued, that I'm about to fall apart.

Swallowing hard, I follow her back to the car. As we walk, my eyes scan the sand dunes, the spaces between the boards, and finally the sandy parking lot. Nothing. My mother's cross is gone. The wind whips my hair into my face and stings my skin. I wish to God that I never came out here with Sean. I lost so much that day, more than I could bear to lose.

I refuse to fall apart. I refuse to succumb to the sensations choking me, to the stabbing pain in my hollowed-out heart. I won't turn to dust. This will not destroy me. I am strong.

Sucking in the cold air, I let it fill my lungs until they ache. I hold it a beat longer than I should and let it out slowly. My breath makes a long, white cloud. My fingers ball up at my sides as I wonder why

I can't give up, why I can't simply fall to the ground and die. I'll survive this, I know I will.

That necklace wasn't holding me together. Something else is—something strong—but I have no idea what it is.

CHAPTER 5

Time passes painfully slow. I stare, not looking, not listening. Lectures blur together and I move through campus like a robot. I smile when I should, wave at my friends, and basically go through the day on autopilot. It isn't until my lab with Marty that he calls me on it.

"Avery," Marty says, leaning in and pinching my arm.

"Owh!" I finally glance at him and actually see him. For the first time since we left the beach, my eyes focus and I actually see him. "What'd you do that for?"

"You're mixing the wrong stuff together. Snap out of it! You've had this glazed over look on your face all day." He watches me for a second.

Surprised, I flinch and look up at him. His brown eyes are like big candies. He's nothing but sweetness and I'm nothing but bitter. "Sorry," I say, and tuck a curl behind my ear. I reach for the lab sheet and confirm my mistake.

"There's nothing to apologize for— well, not unless you blow us to kingdom come. Why don't I do the lab and you fill out the sheet?" I smile weakly at him and sit down on my stool, taking the paper in my hands.

"So," Marty says, his eyes darting over to my seat occasionally, "What are your plans this weekend?"

The corner of my mouth pulls up. It's a lame smile, the kind that covers how stupid I feel. "I'm working." And not getting paid, because I'm an idiot and threw all my money back at Sean. Why did I do that?

I push the thought away, knowing that if I was given the chance for a do-over, I'd repeat the entire night just as it was. Some kind of resolve swirls in my stomach and I feel it creep through my body. I won't live my life halfway. That's why I'd do it all over again. That's why I'm a moron. I'd tell Sean that I loved him, that he scares me to death, and then I'd stand there and wait for him to reject me. Maybe I've got a martyr complex. I rub my fingers against my temples, trying to fight off the headache that's closing around my brain like a vice.

Marty mixes something together. I write down the quantities on my sheet. After a moment, he says, "Ah. Do you know what you're doing, yet?" Marty doesn't look at me. His hands have a slight tremor, or maybe I just imagine it.

I jot down the next answer and say, "No. I've been demoted. So it shouldn't be anything major. Probably a date or something." I tick off a few more things on the sheet. I'm not sure how much Marty knows. Mel filled him in at least a little bit, but he hasn't spoken to me about it.

Marty doesn't look up at me. Maybe it's me, but he seems really tense. His fingers wrap around a beaker and he holds it too tight. The glass shatters in his hand. I jump from my seat at the same time everyone in the class looks up. Marty's fingers uncurl one by one. Streams of blood drip from his palm. Without thinking, I grab my sweater and pull it over my head so that I'm only wearing my tank top and jeans. I take the sweater and brush away the glass that's sticking to the blood on his hand. I grip his wrist tightly and pull his hand up over his heart. Marty watches me, his dark eyes don't leave my face. I don't think. I just react. There's no TA, no prof. I look around the room, but no one offers to help.

I tug Marty away from the lab table, and say, "I'm taking him to the health office. I'll be back to clean that up." No one answers. They watch me lead Marty out of the room.

Marty's eyes are on my hand, watching my hold on his wrist. He swallows hard, like he might faint. I grin at him, suddenly worried about what to do if he does pass out. Marty is way too big for me to carry to the nurse. A hysterical image of me dragging the giant guy by his ankles, through the grass, all the way across campus, pops up in my mind.

I smile and glance at him. "You're not going to pass out, are you? Because I don't think I can carry you. I'll have to drag you to the nurse's office, and I'll probably ruin that shirt you love so much…maybe even nag your head around." I grin at him, but Marty still looks at me with a super weird expression.

We walk down the hallway and I'm trying to hold his wrist up by his shoulder. My sweater is turning red. It's wrapped around his hand. Damn, that's a lot of blood. He must have continued to squeeze the glass after it shattered.

Marty blinks a few times and gets the wry smile on his face that he's usually wearing. He pulls his wrist free from my grip. "I can do that. I'm not going to pass out, either, so stop thinking about rolling me down that hill by the cafeteria."

I laugh nervously. There's something about the look in Marty's eye, the way he won't meet my gaze for more than a second. Marty stops at the exterior door at the end of the hall. I push it open and we walk outside. Glancing in the direction of the hill, I say, "We should do that anyway. I mean, when's the last time you rolled down a hill just for the fun of it?"

"When I was five." He smirks. "Yeah, you're right. It's been too long. If I wasn't hemorrhaging, I'd make you do it now, but alas, I'll have to take a rain check."

"Alas?" I tease. "Really?"

Marty shrugs. "Sure, why not? I think I may speak in medieval talk all day tomorrow. I'll make sure to raise my hand in each class so I get called on. The professors love it when I do that. A few weeks ago I talked like an 80's dude all day. They loved that." Marty blinks hard and grits his teeth. "I think there's glass in my hand."

"Yeah, there is. Don't squeeze it!" I snap at him and make him hold his hand up by his shoulder. His shirt is getting a red blot. The cut must be deeper than it looked. I want to scold him. This seems so stupid, so unusual for him. It almost seems like he did it on purpose. "What made you do that, anyway? This isn't like you." It's not like Marty at all. He's normally meticulous to the extreme. Breaking a glass in his hand was the strangest thing he could do, shy of eating it.

Marty doesn't look over at me, works his jaw and stares straight ahead. "I don't know. It just broke."

Smiling, I say, "Glass doesn't just break—"

"Well, it did. Damn, Avery. Back off. Shit breaks sometimes." Marty keeps walking, taking his long strides, but I stop. He's never spoken to me like that before. Marty is always all gossip and smiles. He never raises his voice. If he swears, it's for drama. He's never sounded like that before. I find myself standing still and my feet won't move.

After a few paces Marty stops. Looking at the dead grass beneath his shoes, he says, "Sorry. I didn't mean to…" His voice trails off. Lifting his gaze slowly, Marty looks at me. There's something there, something that doesn't make sense. He's looking at me with this raw expression on his face, like I was the one who shoved the broken beaker into his hand and made him bleed.

"It's been a rough couple of days." He smiles at me and whatever I thought I saw is gone, concealed behind the mask of smiles and laughter. "I'll take care of this on my own. If you could go back and grab my books, that'd be great. I'll get them from you at breakfast, okay?" Although his tone makes it sound like he's asking me, I know he isn't. For some reason Marty doesn't want me around right now.

Confused, I nod. I wonder what I did that bothered him like this. I can't think of anything, but I don't press him. "Sure. I'll take care of it. Don't worry about anything. I'll finish up the work and turn it in, too. I'll see you in the morning."

Marty nods curtly. He turns and walks away without looking back.

CHAPTER 6

The night seems to take forever. It seems like the sun will never rise. I get up before dawn. I can't sleep anyway. I pull on jeans and a sweatshirt.

As I yank my hair back into a sloppy ponytail, Amber stirs. She groans, "Where are you going, freak? It's not even 6:00am."

"Go back to bed, Skankzilla." I glance at her. Amber isn't really awake. I doubt she'll even remember talking to me. I yank on my sneakers as she rolls back over and disappears under her covers. I wish I could sleep like that, but I can't. I hardly sleep at all anymore. There are too many thoughts racing through my head, too many memories that flash just as I close my eyes. My body aches, tired from lack of sleep—tired from life.

Grabbing my wallet, I shove it in my back pocket, take my book bag, and fish my keys out of my purse. I walk down the hall alone. No one is awake. The kids that stay up forever are passed out somewhere. The only sound I hear is the hum of the florescent lights overhead. Adjusting my bag on my shoulder, I run down the flights of stairs, and push open the door.

Frigid air blasts me in the face. It feels like I walked into a freezer. I welcome the onslaught of sensations, the way the air pricks my skin, stinging it. It reminds me that I'm alive and I need that right now, I need that today.

After getting my car started, I drive to the beach. I'm not searching for the lost necklace today. That's not what this is about. I need to hear the waves and feel the sand. I need the peace that eludes me and I know that I can find it there, despite everything that's happened to me.

The roads are fairly empty once I hit Ocean Parkway. No one goes to the beach this early, not when it's freezing outside. I shiver in my car, as I drive along, watching sea and sand fly by my window. It isn't until I pull into Field 5 and step out of my car that I feel like I can relax a little. It's too cold. I know I can't stay long, but I can't shake the crushing grief. It snuck up on me in the middle of the night and wouldn't let go. For some reason, sitting and watching the waves makes me feel better. This is my security blanket, the one thing that makes me feel better even on the worst days.

I walk onto the sand and head toward the water. Glancing up and down the beach, I see no one. Seagulls screech overhead and fly away when they see I have no food. I sit on the dry sand and stare out at the waves. The sea is smooth today, like a sheet of black glass. It laps at the shore, almost hugging it as if they were friends. Solace finds me and an unexplainable inner-warmth swirls within my stomach.

Everything will be okay.

I stare, unblinking at the sea, allowing the wind to chill my skin until it's numb. I wrap my arms around my knees and pull them to my chest, locking my fingers. I breathe, and blink. Sometimes it's the little things that help me get through the big things. Taking one moment at a time, one breath at a time. It seems manageable, even when my life is not.

The sun is creeping over the horizon, lazily spilling orange and pink streaks across the sky. It isn't until the sun is halfway up that I see someone dressed in a heavy coat down the beach. They're standing so far away that I can't see their face. The man is speck on the horizon, a black dot in a warm coat.

My throat tightens. I react to him. I know it's *him*. I sense it. The wind ruffles his dark hair. The man turns his head as if he can feel my gaze. My heart beats harder. I wish it would still. I wish Sean didn't make me respond this way.

I ignore him. Maybe I'm wrong. Maybe it's some other guy. I can hope. My tongue presses against the back of my teeth as I lock my jaw. I try to relax and ignore the man, but I can't. I stare at the slow waves and the next time I look down the beach, the man is gone. The tension lining my spine softens and I breathe in deeply.

I blink and decide to fall back in the sand. The urge to lay back and look at the sky overwhelms me. Things like the sky and the sea calm me. They remind me how small I am. Maybe that makes other people feel lost, but it makes me feel like maybe my problems aren't so large, like maybe I can really survive this life and all the things that have happened to me. If a grain of sand can stand to be pounded by the sea, then I can take the beating I've been handed.

Sucking in a deep breath, I smile and fall back onto the sand. When I look up, I expect to see the colors of the sunrise painted across the sky, but I don't. I see a man's upside-down face, looking at me. I screech and push up on my elbows, crab-walking away from him a few paces, until my brain registers that he isn't here to kill me—that I know him.

"What the hell, Ferro?" I grab my heart through my sweatshirt. I can't breathe. I don't look up at him. There's something about his eyes that will make me believe whatever he has to say. I can't be here, not with him. Not now.

Sean looks down at me. I can feel his gaze on my cheek. "I apologize. I didn't mean to startle you. I was—"

"Well, what the hell were you doing, standing that close if you didn't mean to startle me? I mean—fuck—could you be any creepier? Damn, Sean." I stand up and brush the sand off my shirt and my jeans. I walk away from Sean before he answers. I don't want to hear it.

Sean's behind me, following me. "Avery, wait. I wanted to tell you—"

But I don't stop. I'll never stop—not for him—not ever again. Sean's mouth is filled with lies. His voice makes deceit sound like music. If I stop, if I look at him, I'm screwed. I'll cave in and hear Sean out and I don't want to. There's nothing he can say that will fix what he's done. He flambéed any chance we had for anything. I walk faster, but my feet just sink into the sand. It fills my sneakers, but I don't stop.

"Avery!" Sean calls behind me. "I need to give this to you. Wait a second."

I hear him running up behind me. As I step onto the boardwalk and off the sand, Sean catches up with me. He manages to grab my elbow. I whirl around, heart pounding. Everything he does puts me on edge. Sean can't speak without my pulse roaring in my ears. My brain registers the touch as pain. My arm sears like he's burned me. I yank it back, hard, and then swing. I throw my shoulder into the punch, not holding back.

Shock flashes across Sean's beautiful features swiftly. My fist is on a collision course with his face. At the last second, Sean steps to the side. My punch lands on his shoulder. He grabs my wrist and holds it tight. Sean looks down at me like I've lost my mind. "What are you doing?"

I try to pull away from him, but he doesn't release me. Every inch of my body is shaking with rage. It courses through my veins and I feel like I'm going to explode. Still, I don't look at his eyes. He's a goddamn snake, a viper. He'll steal my soul and devour me.

I scream in his face without looking higher than his chin. "What am I doing? What are you doing? This is my place, not yours! You have no fucking right to—"

"To what?" He yanks my wrist and pulls me closer, making my body smack into his. The scent of his cologne hits me hard. Vivid memories of his body intertwined with mine flash through my mind. "To what, Avery?" His voice makes me want to cry. The way he talks to me—it sounds like nothing's happened—that he still regards me exactly the same way he did before, and it kills me. It kills me because that means that I meant nothing to him, not before and not now.

I twist my hand out of his grip and pull away. I feel reach toward my shoulder and evade his hand so he can't touch me. "To nothing! Nothing… Just leave me alone." My voice no longer shakes. My neck feels tight like it might turn to stone. I lock my jaw to keep from speaking. I hasten my pace and walk away from him. I hear Sean's expensive shoes following me down the boardwalk. I don't look back. I just walk faster.

"I have something for you." Sean says it like he's going to hand me the piggy kite, like nothing went badly between us. I don't turn back. I don't look over my shoulder when I no longer hear his footfalls inching closer and closer.

I'll never go back to him. He can go to hell.

I manage to start my car and leave without speaking to him. Sean doesn't follow me. I don't see his car. He lets me leave. I don't understand why he was here, why he followed me. I can barely think, so I don't think at all. I don't know why Sean was here, but it doesn't matter. Nothing he does matters anymore.

CHAPTER 7

The rest of the week is more of the same—more sleepless nights, more tension that won't ease out of my muscles, more distance from my friends. Mel watches me closely. It makes me feel brittle, like I'll lose it if she says something to me, so I avoid her for a few days. Marty is even worse. Ever since he broke that test tube in lab, he's become more distant. I wish I knew what I did that made him like this, but I won't ask. I know he won't tell me.

Miss Black called me midweek and told me that I would be an escort this weekend, to show up at her place on Friday night at 6:00pm and she'll go over the details. It's an hour before our meeting. I'm trying to pin up my hair into a loose up-do. I hope it looks sexy and not sloppy. There's a fine line with hairstyles and I'm never really sure which side of the line I'm on.

I slip into my only dress and heels and head for my car. On the way outside, I see Marty walking toward me in the parking lot. His eyes sweep over me and he grins. "Hey, hooker. Got a hot date?"

I smirk in response. "Maybe. And calling me 'hooker' is really weird."

"Yeah," Marty replies, looking at me from under his lashes like he's a big kid. He's all smiles again. It's nice. "I'd rather call you tramp anyway."

I lightly punch his arm and lean into him. I'm surprised when he pulls me in for a bear hug. Crumpling my dress, Marty holds me so tightly that I can't breathe. Whatever made him upset with me seems to be gone. Thank God. I need him. I had no idea how much support he gave me until he was gone. Marty spins me around once and sets me down.

Laughing, I smack his chest. "You ass! You wrinkled my dress. And, if you're going to call me by my nickname, at least get it right. I'm Tramperella. See," I say pointing at my silvery shoes, "glass slippers."

Marty laughs, but there's an oddness to it, like he won't ever call me that. His eyes dart away. "Better get going, right? It's not like you can skip it tonight, is it?"

I shake my head. "No. I have to fix this. I'll see you later. It shouldn't be all night." Marty perks up at that. He smiles, says he'll wait up for me and heads into the dorm to look for Mel. For some reason, she's home tonight. Maybe she has a stash of cash and only works when she runs out. I wish I could plan ahead like that. I kind of suck at planning. Obviously.

I arrive at Miss Black's and take the elevator up to her floor. When I step out, Gabe is standing there. I nearly walk straight into him. "Oh," I say, startled, and step back. "Is Miss Black here?"

The large man nods and says nothing, gesturing for me to go around him. I walk around him slowly and wonder what's going on. As I walk back toward Miss Black's office, I hear her heels clicking on the floor, coming toward me.

"There you are. You're late." Miss Black glances up at me and takes in my outfit. She looks like she's going to have a coronary. "Avery, we've discussed this. You cannot wear the same outfit day after day."

I glance at my dress. "Why not? This is a different client and the dress is clean. I don't smell bad, do I?" My stomach flips as I consider sniffing my armpits. I stop myself and wait for her answer, but Miss Black doesn't dignify me with a response. Instead, she walks swiftly to the wardrobe she has hanging in her office.

When I walk into her office, Miss Black is reaching into the back of her closet. She pulls out a hanger with a dark red dress. It's sleek and long, and from the looks of it, way too small for me. "Wear this. And soon as you work off this debt, you have to purchase your own attire. Is that clear?"

I nod and take the dress. I strip down to my undies and bra before trying to slip into the dress. Black is behind her desk, looking for something. When she glances up at me, she sighs like I'm an idiot. "Lose the bra. It has a built in. Since the client didn't purchase your company for the entire night, the dress code differs."

The red gown is around my hips. I'm trying to shimmy it up as she speaks, but it won't go over my curves. The zipper bites into my thigh. Miss Black stares at me with an expression on her face that makes me nervous. "It doesn't seem to fit." I step out of the dress and look down at the fabric in my hands

She doesn't answer. Miss Black steps around her desk, and takes the dress from my hands. She snaps, "Bra off. Now." She's practically tapping her foot. I have no idea what she's doing. That dress won't fit me. My hips are too wide. I don't have the guts to refuse, and I need to go on this date, so I yank off my bra and drop it on the chair next to me.

"Arms over your head," she says and I pull my hands together on top of my head like I'm going to jump off a diving board. Miss Black manages to slip the gown over my head without messing up my hair. The buttery fabric falls into place, clinging to my curves. "Turn," she snaps. I turn around and Miss Black inches up the invisible zipper on the side of the gown. I can barely breathe, it's so tight.

"There," Miss Black says when the dress is on. "Go look in the mirror behind the door."

I turn from her, walk to the office door, and close it. There's a full length mirror for me to see my entire figure in this dress. When I look at the glass, I can't believe it. I look older, more mature, with more curves than I ever dreamed possible. The dress makes my waist look tiny, while making my boobs look ginormous. Even my hips look perfect in this dress. I'm a bombshell, all feminine curves with each and every one on display.

I can't find my voice at first. I'm shocked. "Holy… this dress is amazing."

"Yes, it certainly is. Come over here." I walk toward her slowly. The gown is fitted and clings to my body. It doesn't flare out until it hits my knee. If I had to chase my car down Deer Park Avenue, I wouldn't be able to run in this thing. It's so clingy.

"This is your date for the evening. His name is Henry Thomas. Normally, we don't divulge full names, but he needed an escort for a business meeting. You are to be cordial and polite. Speak when spoken to, but otherwise you are an ornament—arm candy. Do you understand?"

"Yes."

Miss Black narrows her eyes at me. "If you blow this Avery, you have no place here. There are no more chances, no more do-overs. And, the debt will be taken in a different way, and believe me—you don't want that. So no matter what happens, you are to make sure that Mr. Thomas has a wonderful night."

I nod slowly, wondering how else they'd take the debt. Swallowing hard, I ask, "What if he wants more? I mean, does he know that things are…" I don't know what to call it. "Does he know that there's no sex?"

"Yes, he knows." Miss Black leans her hip back against her desk. "He requested an escort for a business transaction. Your presence makes the meeting have a more social feel, which he thought would benefit both parties. Tension and testosterone often end poorly. Adding a beautiful woman to the mix makes things more palatable.

"If Mr. Thomas requires additional services, they will not be tonight. There are no changes once a contract is executed. You are expected to act familiar, touch his hand or shoulder, kiss him if he deems it appropriate, but that is all. He is aware of the rules. Since, things have gone poorly for you, Gabe will be your driver tonight. He'll be watching you and reporting back to me. If things are not up to par tonight, Miss Stanz—"

I cut her off, understanding her warning. "They will be. I will be everything you expect and more. I promise." She nods, but looks skeptical. After a moment, I ask, "How many times do I have to do this to pay back the money I owe?"

"Too many, Avery. Odds are, you'll have to be promoted to a call girl again to be able to earn that kind of money. If you manage to do well tonight, I'll make it happen. There was a gentlemen here yesterday asking about someone like you."

My heart is stone. The idea of having another man's hands on me doesn't make me shiver anymore. I know what I need to do. I know that I need to steel myself so that I feel nothing. Mel's plan of having fun didn't work. I seem to be monogamous to my core. It's not exactly unexpected, but I'm still surprised. I guess I want what everyone else wants—someone to love. Love and sex aren't the same thing. I know that now. I should have known it before, but that simple fact never fully sunk in.

"Thank you," I manage. *Thank you for letting me be a hooker. Thank you for being my pimp.*

I wonder how I fell so far so fast. If someone told me that I'd be doing this a year ago, I would have laughed in their face. Now, nothing is funny. Truth is like that, sharp as a knife and twice as painful.

Miss Black goes over a few other details about the night, and I'm escorted to the front of the suite where Gabe is waiting for me. Gabe walks to the elevator and presses the button. Miss Black and I stand in silence for a moment. The doors slide open and before I can step inside, she clears her throat. I look back.

"Don't disappoint me, Avery," Miss Black warns, and turns back without waiting for my reply.

CHAPTER 8

Being an escort is different than being a call girl. This is much less nerve racking. Actually, I feel okay, aside from the resentment that's floating in my stomach at having to work for free. But, it's my own fault. I shouldn't have thrown that money back at Sean. It just made everything worse. I'm not even sure what the point was anyway.

No, that's a lie. I knew what the point was and I'm so stupid that I'd do it again. I'm good like that. I don't learn lessons the way I should. My music teacher pointed this out to me when I was in fourth grade. It's not that I couldn't learn, it was that I refused to change my way of thinking. I thought Bach was a whiny bastard—I still do—so I played the music that way. I never learned to see that things aren't always the way I thought they'd be.

I thought Sean would say he loved me. I'm a slow learner.

Maybe it's more than that. Maybe I just like to root for the underdog. I hoped that Sean could overcome whatever was holding him back—guess I was wrong about that. No, I *know* I was wrong. The man is hollow. Every last bit of him is heartless. Sex is sex and nothing more. It reflects how severely broken he really is.

Why is it that I feel the need to fix every wounded person I find? Why do I so carelessly lump guys into the poor puppy dog category? I shouldn't. Some of them like the way they are—and there's my damnation, my weak link—*some* of them. It's like I can't admit that some people don't want to be saved, that they like being broken. Or maybe it's even more malicious than that—maybe they act a certain way on purpose. We all protect our hearts. That part isn't unusual. Sean just…

I banish the thoughts that are plaguing me. They're poison. Sean is gone and I'm better without him. I know this, but I don't feel it inside of me. There's a certainty in knowing the truth. It locks into your bones and you can feel it. I don't feel better off without him, not yet—it's pure cognition that is disconnected from my heart. It's a thought and nothing else.

I glance out the window of the car. The night air is warmer than usual. People fill the sidewalks and linger outside. It's a lovely night with bright stars thrown against an inky sky. The moon is delicately perched like a sliver of silver just over the city.

Gabe drives the car and explains that we are picking up Henry Thomas. "Since your services are as an escort, this arrangement allows you both to keep your private lives private. I pick you up at Black's and then pick him up at the hotel." Gabe is all brute strength. But, he grips the steering wheel and moves through traffic like a ballerina with grace. There are no jerky lane changes, no blaring horn—not from Gabe. He surprises me.

Smiling, I say, "That and pulling up in my normal car would have freaked him out."

Gabe laughs unexpectedly. It's the kind of laugh that sticks in your chest and makes your body heave and cough. He glances at me in the rearview mirror. "You're a funny kid, you know that?"

"Yeah, I tend to make jokes when there's nothing left to laugh about." I smile, but it fades quickly. I suck my bottom lip into my mouth and chew it. The remnants of nervous habits never seem to fade. They poke their heads out at the strangest times.

Gabe stops at a light. He glances up at me in the mirror as he speaks. "Yeah, ain't that the truth?" Something changes. I don't know what, but I see that look in his eyes. Gabe turns in his seat and says more candidly, "Listen, I don't pretend that it's my place, but the boss is kind of miffed at you. I like you. I've liked you since day one, so I gotta say that you need to make sure tonight goes smooth. No hiccups. You owe too much money. Things'll get dirty if you can't work it off, and I don't want that for you. You get what I'm telling you?"

My eyes drift from the mirror. "I get it."

A somber feeling snakes out of my stomach and into every inch of my body. I can't imagine how I could mess up tonight. I'm confident that I won't make a mistake, that tonight will go smoothly.

I was so utterly wrong that it's unfathomable.

CHAPTER 9

The car slows in front of a sleek hotel with hundreds of glowing windows. Gabe tells me that he'll be back and slips out of the car. I slide across the seat to make room for my fake date. From the picture I saw, I know Henry Thomas is in his mid-thirties and all lean muscle. He has that distinct runner's body, complete with trim waist and narrow hips.

In his picture, Henry's arms were folded over his chest. There was a smirk on his lips—like he intends to know my deepest secret and that he'll enjoy teasing it out of me. Henry is an attractive man, although he's older than my normal preference. Since I don't have to sleep with him, I don't mind. I've never really had a relationship with someone so much older than me. All my friends are college age. The oldest is a seventh-year-senior that's coming up on twenty-six. I wonder what Henry will be like compared to the people I know.

Henry steps out of the front doors of the hotel and strides toward the car with that same smirk on his face. I wonder if that smile is always there, so easily strewn across his face?

Gabe says something to him, and Henry inclines his head before the car door opens and he ducks inside. When Henry settles into his seat and looks up, my heart races a little bit. He doesn't look older than me now. His eyes sparkle like sunlight on the sea. The deep gray color is so unusual that I stare at him a beat longer than I should.

He extends his hand and says, "Henry Thomas. Please, call me Henry."

I wrap my fingers around his hand and shake. I nod once. "Allison Stanz." That is my alias tonight. No real names is the normal rule, but since we are supposed to be a couple, it would be difficult to have a conversation—or an introduction to his business associate—without having a first name, so Miss Black said I am Allison.

"It's lovely to meet you, Allison." Henry looks up after Gabe gets back into the car. "Head toward the restaurant, but take your time about it." Gabe nods and pulls into the traffic. Henry looks back at me in my blood red gown. His eyes sweep over me swiftly before landing on my face. "You're a beautiful woman."

I smile slightly and tease him. "You sound surprised."

"Pictures can be deceiving." His lips curl into a boyish grin. "I suppose you hear this a lot, but you honestly took my breath away. I expected…" Henry sighs and runs his hand through his hair. His silvery eyes sweep over me again before he glances at my face, "I don't know what I expected." He laughs. I hear the nerves in his chuckle and want to put him at ease. The jitters don't help either of us.

I place my hand on his and say, "It's okay. I'm glad you're not an ugg-o, either," and wink at him before leaning back in my seat.

Henry laughs. His smile lights up his face, creasing the lines around the corners of his eyes. "Oh, tonight is going to be fun." He rubs his palms together and chuckles again, like he can't wait.

"May I ask what the night entails?" I shift in my seat and smooth my skirt. I can't really breathe in this dress and hope that I won't have to think too hard. There isn't any oxygen going to my brain. I think the gown is shoving all the air into my boobs. I can barely see my lap from here.

"The usual, dinner, dancing, and talking to a complete ass and trying to get him to sell me his patent. You know, nothing too weird." Henry leans back in his seat and lets out a rush of air like he's nervous. "This guy is an arrogant son-of-a-bitch. He's young and I know that's part of it. The guy is a certifiable genius. The technology he came up with is perfect, exactly what my company needs. I just have to get him to sell it to me and not someone else."

"Ah, so tonight is to butter him up? Or do we want to smack him over the head with a frying pan and toss him into the fire? Just tell me what you need and I'm there." I'm half serious, half kidding. I glance up at Henry after smoothing my skirt. For some reason I think it'll help me breathe, even though it doesn't.

There's an easy way about Henry, like he knows how to handle himself most of the time. "You'd whack him for me?" Henry looks up front and asks Gabe, "Did I call the wrong number? Did you people set me up with an escort or a femme fatal?"

"Miss Stanz is not authorized to whack anyone," Gabe says flatly. He doesn't look at us.

"Ah, well, that's brilliant." Henry's voice catches and I hear a wisp of an accent.

"Where are you from?"

"Oxford, originally—England."

I smile at him, at the way he seems certain and uncertain at the same time. It's kind of endearing. "You mean that big island across the pond? Yeah, I know it."

"You've been?" he asks, interest flashing across his face.

"Once, yes. I got to hear the Beatles sing, and eat fish and chips next to Twining's Teashop..." I don't mean to tease him, so I'm not sure why I am. Henry looks confused. "At Epcot." I feel bad two seconds after I say it. "I'm sorry. I'm just kidding. I'm a little nervous."

"Could have fooled me, and a little humor never killed anyone." He winks at me and adds, "Besides, life's too damn short to be dull. Just don't offend Patent Boy and you'll be bloody brilliant tonight. That dress alone is enough to distract him. Listen, at the end of the night, if the man is still foolish enough to withhold his plans, I want you to dance with him and see if you can get him to talk."

I nod slowly. "So, I'm posing as your date—"

"My fiancé."

"Your fiancé," I repeat, and add, "And I'm here to help keep things from turning adversarial, and if all else fails, you want me to try and butter him up?"

"Exactly, love. A good night would be conversation, food, and a deal for that gizmo of his. A bad night would end with Patent Boy running off the way he usually does when things don't go his way. That's where you come in. You just keep him from leaving—apologize for me being ass, and that kind of thing. It's all a game anyway. The man is as aware of that fact as I am."

The car turns a corner and I see the restaurant. "So, keep him there, help him mellow out, and that kind of thing?" Henry nods. "Can I ask you something?"

"Sure, why not."

"Why'd you hire me to do this?" I ask. "It seems like the kind of thing that a friend could have done."

"Maybe," Henry replies, studying my face. I don't feel like his possession. Call girls and escorts don't seem to be his normal kind of thing. "But this way, I am sure to stack the odds in my favor. I heard the man favors New York women, beautiful brunettes, stacked with curves, and a bit of a sassy lip. I think I hit the jackpot. I've never been so glad I called for a girl in my entire life. With any bit of luck, I'll walk out with the deal tonight, and you—my lovely date— will be rewarded."

My heart is pounding and I don't know why. When the car stops, I feel a chill slink down my spine. Glancing at Henry, I ignore the premonition. He's so excited and my job sounds so easy—flirt with the patent man a little bit and make this more of a social gathering. That, I can do.

Henry steps out of the car and I follow. He leans in and whispers in my ear, "I'm serious about the reward. Help me win this guy over and I'll triple your fee."

Smiling at him, I say, "Sounds perfect. Lead the way Mr. Thomas, love of my life."

I'm smiling now. I can't help it. The past week has been so goddamn awful and tonight feels promising. This is something I can totally do and Mel was right about it feeling like a date. This guy has an agenda and needed someone to help him make it happen. I feel perfectly comfortable and take his arm.

Henry kisses me on the cheek. "For good luck."

"Come on, let's get you nailed—I mean, nail that contract." Henry's laughing and so am I.

It feels comfortable, familiar, even though I have no idea who he is. Henry could be some serial killer with really good manners and a sexy accent for all I know.

Gabe comes inside. He's a few steps behind us and passes by to sit at the bar. I'm under observation tonight, but it doesn't make me nervous, not anymore. Now that I know exactly what I have to do, I intend to do it.

Henry walks to the podium at the font of the restaurant. He walks by several people that are waiting and nods at the host. The slim man is older with silvery hair slicked back and big black bushy eyebrows. The permanent scowl on his face is intimidating. It makes me wonder how old patent man is and if I can convincingly flirt with him. The aroma of fine food and yeasty bread fills my head. Blue flames are dancing in a fireplace that extends down an entire wall of the restaurant. It's an amazing thing to see.

Henry smiles at me. I can tell that nervous flitters are racing through him. After a few moments, a waiter comes over and offers to escort us to our table. I follow along with Henry, my hand wrapped around his arm. Eyes fall on me as we move through the restaurant, but I'm not looking at them. Something in front of me has my full attention. My heart pounds violently in my chest, like it wants to pry apart my bones and crawl out.

Glancing around the waiter, I see a man sitting alone at a large table. His eyes are lowered and his head is tipped downward, like he's reading something on the table. Dark messy hair conceals his face, but I know that hair. I know those shoulders and those cheeks covered in light stubble. *This can't be happening*, runs nonstop through my mind. But it is happening and there's no way to stop it. It's like watching a train wreck. You see the two forces speeding toward each other, and they're on a collision course. I swallow hard, trying to keep my pleasant face intact when we stop in front of the table.

Henry steps around the waiter and extends his hand, "Mr. Ferro, good to see you again. When I heard you were delayed in New York, I couldn't believe my luck."

Sean's eyes lift slowly. He has amber liquid in a crystal glass, no ice. When his gaze falls on Henry Thomas, he seems all right, but when his eyes shift to me—*awh, fuck*. It's everything I can manage to stand there and act like nothing is wrong. I'm fucked; like totally, miserably fucked. There's no way tonight is going to turn out well. There is no way that Sean is going to act like he doesn't know me. I told him to screw off the other day at the beach.

I hate Sean in that moment. I want to scream and yell, but I don't. I can't. I stand there with my plastic expression, pulled into a fake smile. Every ounce of dread that flows through my body is hidden by that grin, but it's so fake that it wants to crack like a piece of dried out plastic.

The final straw falling. This will be the end of me. I'll find out what Miss Black intends to do about my debt. I'll find out what Gabe meant in the car earlier. There's no way back, not now—not ever.

Sean stands and extends his hand to Henry and I. "Sit, please make yourselves comfortable. I took the liberty of ordering desserts since the chocolate soufflé here is worth crossing the pond for, is it not?" Sean smiles broadly at Henry.

They chatter more and we are all seated around the little table. A single candle flickers calmly in the center. My eyes fixate on the tiny flame. I wonder if I could knock the thing over and make it look like an accident. Then, I'd need to run to Schenectady and change my name to Mary Higgins or something.

Damn it. What do I do? Why hasn't Sean said anything? My stomach twists tighter and tighter until I feel like I've been turned inside out.

I realize I zoned out and didn't hear half of what they said. Henry is gently touching the top of my hand. "Sweetheart, Mr. Ferro asked you a question."

I blink and my attention snaps to the hand touching mine, then up to Henry's face. I can't look at Sean. I can't. "I'm sorry.

It's rather warm in here." I take a breath and let it out slowly. It would help if I could actually inhale, but I can't. The dress is so damn tight.

"Please, call me Sean." Sean is leaning back in his seat. He looks stunning. The stubble on his cheeks is perfect. His hair has that naturally messy look that I find so appealing, but it's his sapphire eyes that undo me. As soon as I glance up, I regret it, but I can't ignore him any longer. For some reason, Sean hasn't ratted me out—not yet. "And, it is rather stifling in here, Ms. Stanz. There's a balcony around back that overlooks the park. You could walk the terrace and catch your breath, if you need a moment." Sean holds my gaze as he says it. Each word feels like a nail in my throat. I'm transfixed by his voice, lost in his gaze.

I shake the sensations shooting through me away. "I'm all right, although it sounds lovely." I smile at him and find my footing again. I'm worried about him blowing my cover, but I'm not doing a half-assed job and spending the whole night worrying about it. Today's the day that I'll have no regrets. I'll do the best I can and that's all I can hope for.

Henry and Sean order the food. I have no idea how to read the menu, since it's not in English. I've never felt so stupid in my life. Henry leans in when the first plate is brought out and whispers in my ear, "It's squid and snails in a wine reduction. Try it."

I'm not really a seafood person. Are snails considered seafood? They crawl around in fish tanks, so maybe. Either way, I don't like the booger texture when it comes to food that lives in the ocean.

I smile hard and pick up one of the forks. I think it's the right one, but I'm not really sure. There's a thingie on my napkin to hold the snail shell, kind of like pliers. Briefly, I examine them and wonder who makes these things? They're pliers for rich people who like eating slugs in fancy restaurants. Who else would buy them? I poke my fork at the snail.

Sean watches me. The corners of his mouth twitch, like he's amused. "Do you always eat escargot with your salad fork?"

My brows crept up my face at some point, as I tried to figure out what to do with these things. I watch Henry, and pause. That's when Sean speaks. It's obvious that I've never had them.

I smile confidently and try to grab the little beast. "Yes, I find it's easier to rip that sucker out of his shell. Plus salad is for pussies, so no harm using the fork now and letting the waiters carry it away. Am I right?" I pull the snail out of the shell as I'm speaking and pop it in my mouth like it's a French fry, but the texture throws me off. I make a face and nearly choke.

Henry's eyes are about to fall out of his head. He's lifted his glass of wine to his lips and has a horrified look on his face, but Sean laughs. It kills me to hear that sound, but I know what I'm doing with him. I know how to make Sean loosen up and how to make him clam up. I need Sean to feel happy for a little bit, to make this deal with Henry, so I can get the hell away before my life gets any harder.

Dinner progresses and Henry finally relaxes again. He speaks to Sean about anything and everything. We're nearly through with meal and no one has mentioned the contract yet, or the thingie that Sean is selling and that Henry wants to buy. The waiter sets down a hot drink in a tiny cup. I glance at the array of spoons that I have left on the table. Henry continues to speak about something that's so dull that it should be called matte.

Sean taps the little spoon next to the place setting. I smile at him and use it to stir the little cream-colored B into the hot liquid. That's when Sean's mood shifts. Suddenly, he's all business. "I know why you wanted to meet with me Henry, and I can tell you right now that there's no way it's going to happen."

Henry's face goes slack. "Surely you can't mean that. We haven't even discussed what Project 597 could do for us, for you. It's not just the sale of the patent—it's bigger than that." Henry's voice is too tense.

Sean doesn't react well to tension. I sip my hot liquid, but it's so sweet that my lips buckle. Sean's eyes flick up in time to see my face. He forgets himself and smirks. "Not to your liking Ms. Stanz?"

"No, it's fine. Perfect." I return his smirk, but Sean just stares at me. Henry sees it, notices the intensity of his gaze, but says nothing.

"Tell me, Ms. Stanz, do you intend to take Henry's name after the wedding?" The look on Sean's face chokes me. It's as if he reached across the table and wrapped his fingers around my neck. My heart stops. I fall on the floor and die. At least that's what I hope for.

All night Sean's acted like he wasn't going to out me, like he wasn't going to say it, but now I see it in his eyes. This is the segue—the flourish before the grand reveal. Sean knows that Henry hired me, that Henry intended to play him.

I feel my face flush. My eyes drop. My mouth gapes open, but I don't breathe. I can't. The air feels thick, and I know one little breath will make me choke. Placing my sweaty palms on the table, I stand up. "Please excuse me for a moment, gentlemen."

I walk away without explanation.

I float across the floor of the dining room. The voices surrounding me flutter away so that I don't hear anything but a dull buzz of noise. Too many thoughts rush through my mind and I find myself wanting to run. The muscles in my legs twitch, like I'm going to die if I don't. Nerves won't release their hold on me. I feel Gabe's eyes on my back as I walk toward the ladies room, the only place that no one will follow. I need a plan. I need to fix this unfixable mess.

Maybe I should just crawl out the bathroom window. I touch my hand to my forehead and breathe in. *Awh, superfuck. What do I do?* I can't stay here and wait for the other shoe to drop. I can't sit there and watch. The magnitude of this is unimaginable. Everything hinges on tonight.

I can't think.

I reach the ladies room and walk inside. There is no one else here. The room is dark and swankly decorated. It has a powder room feel with little Victorian looking tuffets to sit on and your apply make-up. I step around the fluffy seat and stand in front of the sink. Placing my hands on the cold granite counter, I look up into the mirror and shiver.

I don't know what to do. I don't know how to get out of this. Squeezing my eyes together hard, I blink. Why can't I think? In the moments that really matter, my brain seems to vacate my body, and I'm stuck with this surreal feeling like life is moving in slow motion. I inhale, closing my eyes as I do it. I have to calm down. I have to get a grip on this, either that or run like hell.

When I open my eyes I nearly jump out of my skin. I lift my chin and look up into the mirror expecting to see only my face, but someone else is there—Sean. I never even heard him come in. I grab my heart like it's going to explode.

I want to scream at him. I'm unraveling. I feel the strands popping one by one. Fury rises to the surface and I can't hold it back. Too much has happened between us, too many good things and too many bad things. I round on him. Sean is two steps behind me. I practically jump on him and slam my fists into his chest. I hate my reaction, but I can't stop it.

I speak with a voice that isn't mine. It hisses from between my teeth with too much venom, too much hatred. "Why can't you leave me alone? You're ruining my life, you sick bastard! You think this is funny?

You think that you can just have me and play with my mind, like I don't fucking matter? Well, it's not going to happen—not again you arrogant prick—so walk away and leave me the hell alone."

My fingers are stretched wide as rage races through my veins. I shove Sean again, but he barely moves. It feels like my heart's become a black hole and my entire body is being crushed and sucked into the massive force. My chest aches, it literally aches to have him so close.

Instead of leaving, Sean grabs my wrists so I stop hitting him. Fury makes my body tremble. It's like the hissy fit he just witnessed was the smoke before the real eruption. Sean's cool eyes sweep over my face. His grip on my arms loosens. I pull back, but my muscles won't stop twitching.

Sean's lips part like he's going to say something, but the words won't leave his mouth. He breathes strangely, like I punched him in the gut and he looks at me with those liquid blue eyes. Somehow he makes me feel sorry for defending myself, for telling him off.

Screw this. I am not so fucked up that I'm going to feel sorry for this. I turn to leave and walk quickly for the door. Without looking back, I say over my shoulder, "Do whatever the hell you want. You're good at that." My hand is on the cold doorknob when he speaks.

"Avery, I have no intention of telling him anything. I simply meant to—"

I stop. My fingers practically strangle the doorknob. I cut him off, not giving him a chance to fully state anything. "I don't care."

"I need to tell you something, but every time I approach you—"

"I still don't care," I say back. The words come from within the hollowness. I feel them rattle through me before they spill out of my mouth. "I don't care about anything you have to say and I don't care about you. I hate you. I hate what you've done to me." My eyes narrow to slits and I turn around.

Suddenly, I'm in his face saying the things I wish I'd said the night he sent me away. "I hate that you're so damn callous. I gave you my heart and you fucking returned me. Nothing you can say will ever fix that. I have no interest in what makes you tick, or why you followed me in here. You can go to hell."

Sean reaches into his lapel and pulls out an envelope. It's thick, like it has lots of paper inside. "This isn't mine."

I stare at him and his envelope of cash. I hope he knows every thought that races through my mind. I hope he knows how much he hurt me and how much I wish I'd never met him. I feel my lips move and words start to pour out. "Oh, it's yours all right. Don't you know how returns work? You get your money back. You got me for free—"

"This isn't about the money, but you're wrong and need to take it. I—"

"You don't get to have a say in anything I do. I'm not taking that back. It's tainted. This is the end of this conversation. Go ahead and do whatever amuses you. I know you will." I turn away sharply, but Sean manages to grab my wrist.

He pulls me back to him, hard, too hard. I smack into his chest and he holds onto me tightly. Sean steps forward and before I know it, he has me pressed against the wall. It seems like hours have passed since I walked into this room. How is it that no one else has come in? And if they come in now, it looks really bad.

Sean's lips are too close to mine. A wave of his warm breath drifts across my cheek and I shiver. I'm paralyzed, unable to move. I don't know what's doing it—if fear has me so scared that I can't move or if it's something else, something I don't even want to consider.

When Sean speaks, something inside me reacts and I melt. "You think this amuses me? You think that I don't know what I've done to you? You really think that it makes me happy?"

I don't answer. He's too close. My mind can't process all the emotions racing through my body. My veins are on fire and someone has stolen every last breath from my lungs. I shiver, and Sean holds me tighter. My eyes are locked onto his. Neither of us speaks. His lips, those perfectly pink lips, part like he wants to say more—like he wants to kiss me—but Sean doesn't move. He's frozen. My heart pounds harder, faster. Buzzing fills my ears and my knees go weak.

After a moment, Sean forces himself to blink. From under those thick dark lashes, he says, "I made a mistake. I don't know—"

Something inside me snaps. His words ignite strength within me and I pull away, saying, "You've made too many mistakes. I can't do this with you. I don't know what you need, or who you really are. I'm not even sure if you really know, but this," I gesture between us, "is a bad idea. It's like setting a cigarette down on an open keg of gunpowder. It's not a question of whether or not it'll explode, it's a question of how much damage it will it do when it does blow up, and with you—I already know that answer.

"I gave you everything I had and you sent me back. I'll be the trash you think I am. I'll become what you made me. But, I will never, ever, come groveling back, asking for your affection or your friendship. And you know why? Because there's nothing left in here," I ball my hand into a fist and hold it over my heart. "There's nothing left but a shell and I know that one wrong move—just one more—will be the end of me, and I have no intention of allowing that to happen—especially not with you."

My voice is too calm. The way I say it is completely detached, like I'm reporting on someone else's life, someone else's soul. I watch his eyes and the way he drinks me in, but I feel nothing. The longer I speak, the more emptied out I feel. I turn and walk back to the door, numb with shock.

Sean's voice is soft, apologetic almost, "I made the deal with Henry. I did it for you."

His confession doesn't make me pause. It doesn't change anything. Without a word, I push through the door and walk away.

CHAPTER 10

Henry is beaming at me and won't shut up once we're back in the limo. "Do you know how many people wanted that patent and I'm the one who got it! Do you know what this means?" If he smiles any wider, his teeth will fall out of his head. Henry is practically bouncing in the seat next to me. "And it's all because of you! I know it! Ferro has a weakness for beautiful women. I saw him walk away shortly after you left the table. Did he talk to you?"

I glance at Henry out of the corner of my eye. I don't want to talk about it, so I smile and shake my head. "No, not really. I saw him after I left the ladies room."

Henry looks at me for a moment and then reaches for his wallet. "I told you that I'd reward you and I'm keeping my promise." He fishes out some larger bills and counts them swiftly.

Lifting my hand, I stop him. "I can't take tips. You'll have to give it to Miss Black."

"But I want you to have it." Henry looks at me with a childlike expression.

I assure him that I'll get it, that it'll help me, before Gabe drops him off at his hotel. Henry finally puts his money away. Then, he exits the car, jumps in the air, and whoops. His happiness is contagious. I can't help it. I smile at him and wish him well. He seems like a good guy.

At the last second, Henry turns back to the car and asks, "If I were to ask you on a date—"

My eyes drop to my hands when he asks. "I'm not allowed to date."

"At all?" he asks, stunned. I shake my head and smile at him. "So, if I want to see you again…?"

"You have to order me." *That sounds really weird.*

Henry leans on the car at the open window. "Would you like to see me again?"

He's flirting with me. It makes me smile. I can't believe this guy. "I would love to see you again, and I'd love to hear what you plan on doing with that patent. I can tell it means a lot to you."

"It does!" He's all happiness and rainbows. I wouldn't be surprised if a unicorn shot out of his ass—he's that happy. "I'll set it up and I'm telling your boss that you're exceptional, because you are. No one can tame Ferro and somehow, you did! It's amazing. You're an amazing woman and I can't wait until our next date." He's grinning so wide. Henry turns around and dances a gig as he walks away from the car. I wonder how long it'll take him to fall asleep tonight. He got everything he wanted.

As we pull away from the curb, Gabe says, "You have the shiftiest luck, you know that, right?"

My eyes flick up to the mirror. "I'm well aware."

"What were the odds of Ferro showing up? I mean, I don't know how you kept that whole situation from blowing up, but you did. I'm telling Black that it's not you. Whatever occurred between you and Ferro in private, whatever happened, is on him. She should reinstate you in time to fuck Henry's brains out next weekend. That should fix your financial problem with Black and you'll be back on the books again."

I stare out the window as he speaks. My lips are parted and I breathe slowly. This is my life. I'm a call girl. I'll get to be with someone else and wash the vivid memories of Sean away. I nod slowly. This is what I wanted. Somehow, I survived the night and made a positive impression on Gabe and Henry without making things worse with Sean.

Gabe speaks, pulling me from my thoughts. "You've got that stormy look in your eye."

"Excuse me?" I've never heard that expression before and I'm not sure what he means.

"It's like your mind is a sea during a storm. I see it in your eyes. You need to hide that. It means people can still get at you, take bits and pieces away, and from the looks of it you don't have much to give."

I stare at Gabe, wondering if I'm always so transparent. I thought I did a good job hiding everything. Maybe not. Instead of replying, I nod.

Gabe drops me off at Black's and I go upstairs. I file my report and turn in my gown. I put on my old dress and tie my Chuck's back on my feet. I toss my purse and heels into a bag and head for the elevator. When the doors open, Gabe is standing there. He holds the door for me. "You did well, kid. No worries. You still got this job."

"Thanks," I say, and the doors slip shut.

When I exit the building, it's late. I grab a can of ether and start my car. It rumbles to life and for the first time in a long time, I wish I had a coat. Shivering, I drive back home, but I take the long way getting there. I drive past the dark beach. The scent of salt water fills my head as the wind blasts my face through the window. Eventually, my skin becomes numb. I wish I could stay like that. I wish I didn't feel every goddamn thing. For a moment, I'm jealous of Sean, of his ability to shut me out so thoroughly. I wish I could do that.

By the time I get off the parkway and head down Deer Park Avenue, I'm totally frozen. My icy fingers grip my steering wheel as I stop at the light from hell. I rev the engine and keep my other foot on the brake. I glance around. It's a nice night, but it's cold.

My RPMs slip and I feel the car convulse. It's trying to stall. I give it more gas and stop looking around. I try to get the engine to keep running, but it doesn't. The beast shutters and dies. Of course the light changes right then. Horns start to blare. I flip on my hazards and grab the can of ether. After walking around to the front of the car, I open the hood and spray.

While I do, I hear a motorcycle inching closer and closer. It's as if the rider slowed down just to talk to me. My heart races faster. It can't be him. I slam the hood down and see Sean on the shoulder, stuck a few cars back. I know it's Sean, even though I can't see his face. Seeing him makes my throat constrict. It's like someone has a belt and is pulling it tighter and tighter around my neck.

Just breathe and drive away, I tell myself.

After I get back inside, I start the car. It rumbles to life just as I see Sean inching towards me in the shoulder. I don't want to talk to him. I can't. Even though the light is changing to yellow, I gas it. I need to get away from him.

The next few seconds are frozen. They don't pass the way they should. My car has the acceleration of a sloth and I basically start to roll into the intersection. The bike engine revs behind me, growling like a bear. Sean's going to gun it and try to catch me. I don't look back. I press the accelerator pedal down to the floor, and my car starts to pick up speed, but then Sean's bike cuts me off. A red taillight streaks in front of me and I break hard.

I don't see the truck until that moment. Its horn blares as it comes into the intersection. My foot slams on the break and I skid until the rims of my tires slam into the curb. I clutch the steering wheel and watch in horror as Sean tries to evade the massive amount of steel barreling down on him. He turns sharp, but the back tire doesn't grip. It slides out from under him. The bike tips over and falls to the ground. Sparks fill the air like fireworks when the bike's on its side.

Sean hits the pavement hard and rolls uncontrollably into traffic.

I hear a voice screaming, and don't realize that it's me. I'm running. Suddenly, I'm running into the intersection. Sean's bike collides with the side of the truck and bits and pieces of plastic and metal are launched in a thousand different directions. I can't feel anything but my heart beat. It slams into my ribs over and over again. My scream continues to fill my ears, sounding like an echo. I fall on my knees next to Sean's crumpled body. I watched him skid when he hit the ground. I saw the way his neck moved, the way his helmet bounced against the cement like a stone. I'm next to him, calling his name, trying to pull up his visor, trying to see if he's all right. But I know he's not. I already know he can't be.

My mind replays the events and terror fills my veins. He saw the truck. It would have hit me. Sean saw the truck and did this on purpose.

He saved me.

I scream at Sean, calling his name, but he doesn't move. His black jacket and gloves are shredded. There's blood dripping from inside his helmet. I try to unfasten the chin strap, but I can't get it. I'm shaking so badly. I keep saying his name, telling him that it'll be all right.

My hands are on his chest, but I'm scared. I'm so scared that I've lost him. I don't understand how he could do this. I don't understand him at all, and now that chance is gone.

People race around us. Suddenly, I'm not alone. Lights flash around me, bright red and white. They try to take me away from Sean, but I won't go. They pull me from him and force me into the back of an ambulance. The world rushes by in a blur of sounds and colors. There are too many people and not enough cars on the road. Police and paramedics are there. One minute I was alone and the next they were there, trying to tell me to leave Sean's side. They made promises that I've heard before, promises that a person can't possibly keep. They say he'll be fine, but I saw Sean fall and I know.

Memories of the past and the present collide together. I can't even blink anymore. Hands force me down onto a gurney and I lean back. A woman is above me, speaking soothingly, but my heart pounds too hard to hear her.

Finally, her voice cuts through the buzzing in my mind. It's my name, she says my name. The woman smiles at me and dabs my brow with a cloth. "You're hurt, Avery. Let us help you and everything will be okay. Take some deep breaths for me." She speaks with authority, like she knows me. I don't remember telling anyone my name, but she knows it.

I nod slowly and stop fighting them. I'm so tense, so scared. I don't know what will happen. Tears fall from the corners of my eyes and they won't stop. I don't sob or scream anymore. They ask me what hurts and I can't tell them, because I don't understand what's happening to me. One moment I'm fine. One moment I've decide to walk away from Sean, to cut him out of my life, but then he does this.

"He saved me," I manage to say. The ambulance is moving and I don't even remember when the doors closed. The woman looks down at me. There are other faces watching, people I don't recognize.

"Everything will be all right. Believe that." The way she says it makes my head hurt. Suddenly, I can feel things again. My palms burn and it feels like someone cracked my skull open with a bat. It throbs in a way that I've never known. I wince and they add some clear bag to the IV that someone put in my hand.

The rest of the night passes in a blur. I'm sent to the emergency room. People ask questions and I try to answer. I keep asking about Sean, but no one will tell me. I haven't even seen him, yet. He arrived right before me is all they will say. I have this horrible sinking feeling in my chest. I'm drowning, unable to stop.

"Miss Stanz?" a voice says before entering behind my curtain. They've already tended to me. I have a few scrapes on my face and some stiches in my forehead. I'm lucky. I glance up at her. My hands still shake. My throat aches and I can't speak. "Here are your boyfriend's things. He doesn't have an emergency contact or a next of kin on his file." She explains to me and then hands me his torn jacket and busted up helmet. It feels like someone is squeezing my heart.

I take the items and hold them tightly. The nurse slips away and I wrap Sean's jacket around me. Something inside the lapel pokes me. I reach my hand in and pull out an envelope. It's the one he was trying to give me. Sniffling, I pull it out and look at it. Running my thumb over the paper, I expect it to be smooth, but it's not. There's something else in there.

I open the envelope and look inside. There between the envelope and the cash, is a silver glittering necklace and a note. My lower lip trembles as I pull out my mother's necklace. I flip open the note.

I know how much this means to you. I wish I could show you what you mean to me. I messed up, Avery. You'll never know how sorry I am, how much I wish I hadn't said those words. -Sean

I clutch the note to my chest and feel too much. I always feel too much. Horror slips over me, choking me until I can't breathe. Slowly, I fall onto my side, holding his note to my chest like it's a lifeline, like it can change everything.

Memories flash through my mind from the night my parent's died. It was chaos, like this. It was pain and agony, laced with shock and shadows. I couldn't process what was happening, but now I know it—I feel it. My world is caving in. My life is being torn apart again and it's my fault.

This is my fault.

If I'd let him speak, if I didn't keep running away from him, this wouldn't have happened. And it kills me, because that's the point—this was preventable. If I'd spoken to Sean, I wouldn't have driven into the intersection. I wouldn't have run the light. I wouldn't have made Sean cut in front of me. I wouldn't have made him fall. Images of his body hitting the ground play through my mind. They don't stop and I know they never will.

I close my eyes for a moment and curl into a ball. Machines beep behind me. The IV in my hand aches. My whole body aches, but sleep paws at me anyway. The medicine makes me tired. I hear their voices around me.

"She finally drifted off."

"Poor thing. She's been hysterical for…"

And then there's nothing but blackness.

THE ARRANGEMENT SERIES

This story unfolds over the course of multiple short novels. Each one follows the continuing story of Avery Stanz and Sean Ferro.

To ensure you don't miss the next installment, text **AWESOMEBOOKS** to **22828** and you will get an email reminder on release day.

MORE ROMANCE BOOKS BY
H.M. WARD

DAMAGED

DAMAGED 2

SCANDALOUS

SCANDALOUS 2

SECRETS

THE SECRET LIFE OF TRYSTAN
SCOTT

And more.

To see a full book list, please visit:

www.SexyAwesomeBooks.com/books.htm

CAN'T WAIT FOR H.M WARD'S NEXT STEAMY BOOK?

Let her know by leaving stars and
telling her what you liked about
THE ARRANGEMENT VOL. 4
in a review!

Made in the USA
San Bernardino, CA
28 September 2013